Romantic **Meg March** is thrilled when she's asked to sing at Lily Prescott's wedding. Meg practices with extra care because she loves the bride and wants the celebration to be beautiful. But as soon as Meg meets the groom's much younger sister, Julia Thorpe, the two girls clash. Meg can't believe that Julia dislikes Lily, and she is angry when Julia changes the wedding song seconds before the ceremony. What's worse, when the wedding couple departs for the honeymoon, Julia comes to stay with the Marches!

Meg watches as Julia charms her sisters—as she seems to take Meg's place in their hearts. It's time for a confrontation that will make Meg and Julia enemies for life—or turn enemies into special friends.

PORTRAITS
of LITTLE WOMEN

Meg Makes a Friend

Don't miss any of the
Portraits of Little Women

PORTRAITS
of LITTLE WOMEN
*Meg Makes
a Friend*

Susan Beth Pfeffer

DELACORTE PRESS

Published by
Delacorte Press
Bantam Doubleday Dell Publishing Group, Inc.
1540 Broadway
New York, New York 10036

Library of Congress Cataloging-in-Publication Data
Pfeffer, Susan Beth.
    Portraits of Little women, Meg makes a friend / Susan Beth Pfeffer.
        p.   cm.
    Based on characters found in Louisa May Alcott's Little women.
    Summary: Meg is thrilled to be asked to sing at a friend's wedding,
until she meets the groom's sister and they become instant enemies.
    ISBN 0-385-32580-0
    [1. Weddings—Fiction. 2. Friendship—Fiction. 3. Sisters—Fiction.
4. Family life—New England—Fiction. 5. New England—Fiction.
I. Alcott, Louisa May, 1832–1888. Little women. II. Title.
PZ7.P44855Pmm   1998
[Fic]—dc21   97-27855
                                                                         CIP
                                                                          AC

The text of this book is set in 13-point Cochin.

Cover and text design by Patrice Sheridan
Cover illustration copyright © 1998 by Lori Earley
Text illustrations copyright © 1998 by Marcy Ramsey
Activities illustrations copyright © 1998 by Laura Maestro

Manufactured in the United States of America

April 1998

10   9   8   7   6   5   4   3   2   1

BVG

FOR RHODA POLLOCK

CONTENTS

CHAPTER 1

"Oh, Meg," said Amy March. "You look so pretty in your brand-new dress."

"Do I?" Meg asked. It was so hard to tell. The only mirror the March family owned didn't encourage vanity. She moved a few more inches away from it so that she could see more of her new dress.

"Blue poplin," Amy said. "You'll be the prettiest girl at the wedding."

"The bride's supposed to be that," said Jo.

"But Meg will be the prettiest girl not getting married," Beth declared.

Ten-year-old Meg turned from the mirror

and looked at her three younger sisters. Jo, as always, had ink smudges on her face and hands. Beth, two years younger than Jo, was by her side. And Amy, the youngest of the four, was staring with open admiration and envy at Meg in her new dress.

"To think you're going to a wedding," said Amy. "I wish I'd been invited."

"I'm sure Lily Prescott would have invited you if she could have," Meg said. "But since the wedding is at her parents' home and not at church, she had to limit the number of guests."

"You *will* tell us all about it?" Beth said. "We'll want to hear every single detail."

"Don't leave a thing out," said Jo. "I can always use a good wedding scene in one of my plays. Maybe someone will rush in and declare a reason why they can't be wed. A mad wife in the attic or some such thing."

"I'm certain Mr. Thorpe doesn't have a mad wife in the attic or anyplace else," Meg said. "Marmee and Father would have learned about it long ago and warned Lily."

"But tell us everything anyway," said Amy. "What all the guests wear."

"And what the bride's dress looks like," Beth said. "And how she acts."

"And what the food is like," said Jo. "If there isn't to be a mad wife in the attic, at least describe every dish of the wedding feast."

"Are you terribly nervous?" Beth asked.

Meg nodded. "I've never sung at a wedding before."

"That's because you've never been to a wedding before," Jo said.

"Yes, but I wouldn't be so nervous if I were just a guest," replied Meg. "I don't think being a guest could be that much different than going to church. But to be asked to sing, to know all the wedding guests will be listening to me, and I won't know most of them and they won't know me—that truly is frightening."

"Would you like to rehearse again?" Beth asked. "I'm sure there's time before you have to go."

"I'd love to," Meg said. She bent over to

3

give Beth a kiss. "You must be terribly tired of playing 'Amazing Grace' over and over again."

"It's a wonderful hymn," said Beth. "And you sing it so beautifully. I know all the guests will want to burst into applause."

"They mustn't do that," Amy said. "How would Lily feel?"

"She probably won't even be aware," said Jo. "I've read lots of stories about brides, and they all are terribly nervous on their wedding days. Of course in most of the stories it turns out the groom has a mad wife locked in the attic, so the poor brides have cause for their nervousness."

"No one will ever lock me in an attic!" Amy declared. "No matter how mad I might be."

"What a temptation," said Jo. "Come, Bethy. Play 'Amazing Grace' one more time. I do like to hear Meg sing it."

The girls walked downstairs to the parlor, where the March family kept their piano. It was an old instrument and not in very good condition, but Beth could coax tunes out of it as though it were a concert grand.

She began playing the simple hymn, and Meg sang the words perfectly. Lily Prescott had told her that "Amazing Grace" was Mr. Thorpe's favorite hymn and she knew he would be pleased to have it sung.

Meg personally didn't think of it as a wedding sort of hymn, but she supposed the important thing was that Lily thought it would make Mr. Thorpe happy. They were a very romantic couple, in Meg's opinion. Lily Prescott's parents had known Marmee and Father for many years, and the two families had spent many happy afternoons together. It had been on one of those afternoons, shortly before Lily had become engaged to Mr. Thorpe, when she'd heard Meg singing. "I want you to sing at my wedding," she'd said, and Meg, who hadn't suspected that such a wedding might take place, had cheerfully agreed.

A few weeks later an invitation had arrived for Marmee, Father, and Meg to attend the wedding of Lily Prescott and William Thorpe. Meg knew she had been invited so that she could sing, and she wasn't surprised when, the next time she saw Lily, the bride-to-be made that request. Of course Meg agreed, and now, in just an hour, she and her parents would be leaving for the wedding, where she would be singing Mr. Thorpe's favorite hymn.

With all that on her mind, it was a miracle that Meg remembered every word of the song. Of course it helped that she and Beth had rehearsed it endlessly for the past week.

"You *will* promise not to sing it for a little while after today," said Jo, and when Meg's other sisters joined her in that plea, Meg realized how tired they must be of it.

"I promise," she said. "Oh, Beth, I do so wish you were coming. I'd be far more comfortable if you were accompanying me."

"I'm sure Mr. Thorpe's sister will be an excellent pianist," said Beth. "And the piano at the Prescotts' is so much finer than ours."

"But no one can make sweeter music than you," Meg said. "Isn't that true, Father?"

"It certainly is," Mr. March said, coming into the parlor. "But I suppose we must give the sister of the groom her chance to shine.

How do I look, girls? Am I a respectable wedding guest?"

"No one will be handsomer," said Jo.

"It feels strange to be attending a wedding as a guest and not as a minister," Mr. March said. "But Mr. Thorpe is apparently related to Judge Cabot and wished him to preside over the wedding."

"I like the idea of sitting next to my husband at a wedding," said Marmee as she entered the room. "The wedding will be even more special for me because you'll be my escort."

"Marmee, you look beautiful," Meg said. She knew her mother had forgone a new dress so that she might have one. But even in her old silk, Marmee was the most beautiful woman Meg had ever known.

"You do look lovely, my dear," Father said, and he kissed Marmee's hand. "Come, Meg. It is time for the Marches to march on!"

CHAPTER 2

Fortunately for the Marches, their neighbors the Emersons were also good friends of the Prescott family and had invited the Marches to ride in their carriage to the wedding. Father and Marmee and Mr. and Mrs. Emerson chatted away the entire ride, while Meg sang "Amazing Grace" over and over again in her mind.

They arrived at the Prescott house in about twenty minutes. When they got out of the carriage, Meg could see many other guests arriving. All the women wore lovely silk gowns. Meg wished, not for the first time, that her poplin was silk, but even if they could have afforded it, Marmee didn't believe silk was appropriate for young girls. Meg dreamed of the day when she would be old enough to wear it, and beaux would admire her, and one would fall in love with her. Someday, I'll be the bride, she told herself, smiling at the thought.

"Our Meg looks as beautiful as any bride," said Father.

"That she does," said Mr. Emerson.

Meg knew they were being gallant and didn't really mean it, but she didn't care. Everyone agreed Lily had looked lovelier once her engagement had been announced. They would say the same thing about Meg when the time came.

"Look how beautiful the house is," Marmee whispered to Meg.

Meg nodded in silent amazement. The Prescotts had decorated their entire parlor with flowers. There were endless vases filled with deep red roses, and ferns and daisies stood on the fireplace mantel. In addition, the tables had vases with pink clover in them. It was like walking into a splendid garden.

The drawing room where the wedding was to be held was actually rather dark. The Marches kept their house filled with light, but Meg was used to darker, more formal rooms because of Aunt March. Her house always looked as though a funeral could be held there on a moment's notice. But even the more somber drawing room had its share of flowers to brighten the spirits.

Meg walked over to the piano and wished yet again that Beth were there to play for her. She had never met Mr. Thorpe or his sister and knew only what Lily had told her about them. They were orphans, and Mr. Thorpe had raised his much younger sister. The sister's name was Julia; she would be living with Lily and Mr. Thorpe after they were married, and she played the piano.

"She knows 'Amazing Grace' quite well," Lily had assured Meg. "She plays it for her brother nearly every evening."

Still, Meg wished she had had the opportunity to rehearse with Julia. "Amazing Grace" was "Amazing Grace" no matter who played

10

it, she supposed, but it wouldn't have hurt to have gone through it once before the wedding.

"Ah, Meg," said Mr. Prescott as he noticed her by the piano. "You look lovely, my dear."

"Thank you, sir," Meg said.

"Are you ready for your big moment?" he asked. "I know how much Lily is looking forward to hearing you sing."

"I've certainly practiced," Meg said. "I was wondering where Julia Thorpe is. Perhaps I might meet her before the ceremony begins."

"Certainly," Mr. Prescott said. "An excellent idea. She's in the morning room. Why don't you join her there?"

Meg thanked him and walked to the morning room. Although no other guests were there, it too had been decorated with roses and daisies. Half hidden behind a huge vase filled with ferns stood a girl about Meg's age.

"Are you Julia?" Meg asked.

The girl left the protection of the ferns and moved closer to Meg. Meg noticed how pretty the girl would have been if she hadn't had such a sullen expression on her face. Her

11

gown, Meg noticed, was silk. No one had told her she was too young to wear it.

"And what if I am?" the girl said. "Who are you?"

"Meg March," Meg said. "You're to accompany me on the piano."

"Oh, am I?" Julia said.

Meg blushed. "I'm sorry," she said. "All I meant was, Lily Prescott said you played 'Amazing Grace' beautifully, and she asked me to sing it. She did tell you, didn't she, that we were to perform it together?"

"She mentioned something about it," Julia said. "But not 'Amazing Grace.'"

"What do you mean?" Meg asked. "I was told 'Amazing Grace.'"

"I don't care what you were told," Julia said. "My brother told me to play 'Lilly Dale' for the wedding."

"'Lilly Dale'?" Meg repeated.

"Do you know the song?" Julia asked. "It's very popular."

"I've heard the girls at school sing it," Meg said. "But it isn't a hymn."

"William doesn't care if it's a hymn or not," Julia said. " 'Lilly Dale' is his favorite song because his fiancée's name is Lily. And he specifically requested that I play it at his wedding. If you want to sing the words to 'Amazing Grace' while I play 'Lilly Dale,' I'm sure I won't be the one to seem the fool."

Meg couldn't remember ever meeting such a disagreeable girl. "I'm not sure I know the words to 'Lilly Dale,' " she said. "But if you have the sheet music, I suppose I could sing along. I know the tune."

"Then that will have to do," said Julia. "I have the music here. I was looking it over one last time."

"May I look at it?" Meg asked when Julia made no effort to share the music with her.

"If you have to," Julia said.

Meg reached over and took the music from her. She skimmed the lyrics to the song. It was a very sad song, and not one Meg would have chosen for her own wedding. But she supposed grooms had different tastes about these things than brides. And it

was romantic that the song he chose had the bride's name in it.

"Your brother must love Lily a lot," Meg said.

"I suppose," Julia said. "There's no need for him to marry for money."

"That's good," Meg said. "I know how happy Lily is. You must be looking forward to life with her."

"I'm not marrying her," Julia said. "My brother is."

"But she'll be living in your home," Meg said. "You're very fortunate. She's very kind."

"I don't need kindness from her or anyone," Julia said, and she snatched the sheet music from Meg. "Come on. Let's get this performance over with."

CHAPTER 3

*M*eg walked out with Julia and waited as Julia positioned herself at the piano. Meg watched the wedding guests taking their seats and sensed their excitement.

Meg still couldn't understand why anyone would want a song about some girl who had died to be sung at a wedding, but Marmee had often told her there was much about marriage a young girl shouldn't be expected to understand. And if this was Lily Prescott's favorite song, then it was sure to make her happy, and that was the important thing.

Judge Cabot, whom Meg had met once at

Aunt March's, stood at the front of the drawing room. He cleared his throat, first softly and then with considerably more emphasis. The guests stopped whispering to their companions.

Julia began playing the piano. Meg bent over her shoulder and began singing the sad song.

" 'Twas a calm, still night
And the moon's pale light
Shone soft o'er hill and vale
When friends mute with grief
  stood around the deathbed
Of my poor lost Lilly Dale."

Meg could hear murmurings in the audience, but there was no way to stop now. Julia, if anything, played more loudly and insistently.

"Oh! Lilly, sweet Lilly, dear Lilly Dale
Now the wild rose blossoms o'er her little
  green grave
'Neath the trees in the flow'ry vale."

Meg was positive she heard snickering as she sang the song's sad chorus. She looked for her parents and saw Marmee smiling encouragingly at her. Father seemed perplexed, and Mr. Emerson was clearly trying not to laugh.

" 'I go,' she said, 'To the land of rest,
And ere my strength shall fail,
I must tell you where,
    near my own loved home,
You must lay poor Lilly Dale.' "

Meg sang the chorus again, making a point of not looking anywhere except at the sheet music. She hoped Julia would be satisfied with the first and second verses, but she kept on playing.

" 'Neath the chestnut tree,
Where the wild flow'rs grow,
And the stream ripples forth thro' the vale,
Where the birds shall warble
    their songs in the spring
There lay poor Lilly Dale."

18

Julia played the final chorus as Meg sang it one last time. When the girls finished, Meg noticed a great deal of coughing in the audience. She blushed, didn't bother to thank Julia (as she and Beth had rehearsed her doing), and made her way to her parents' side.

"That was lovely, dear," Marmee said.

Father and Mr. Emerson both coughed loudly. Mrs. Emerson shushed them.

Meg tried concentrating on the wedding after that. It took her a few moments to settle down, since she still felt embarrassed, but soon she was watching with rapt attention as the bridesmaids and groomsmen walked down the aisle. Next it was Mr. Thorpe's turn. He seemed like a very pleasant young man, and he had a smile on his face that proved how happy and excited he was on his wedding day.

Then came Lily Prescott, escorted by her father. She had on the most magnificent dress Meg had ever seen. It was white satin, trimmed with row after row of Brussels lace. At the front of the skirt was a huge white bow, and near the bottom was another white bow.

The sleeves were also made of rows of lace, and at the shoulders were more white satin bows. The veil was white tulle with entwined white ribbons. And the wreath on Lily's head was made of orange blossom and jasmine.

People gasped with pleasure at the beautiful bride. Meg felt a strong sense of relief that Lily Prescott looked so healthy. She felt somehow that singing about a dead Lily might sicken the real one.

Judge Cabot recited the wedding ceremony in a deep, somber voice. Lily and Mr. Thorpe gave the called-for responses, and Mr. Thorpe slipped the wedding ring on his bride's finger. He then lifted her veil and exchanged a kiss with his new wife. Meg thought it was quite the most romantic thing she had ever seen.

The other guests must have thought so too, for there was a general sense of delight at the close of the ceremony. Meg noticed Marmee and Father holding hands. She wondered what their wedding must have been like. It had been less costly, she was sure, but no less magical.

As the guests got up and moved to congratulate the new couple, Meg took Marmee aside. "I wanted to sing 'Amazing Grace,'" she said, "but Julia told me to sing the other song instead."

"Don't worry about it, dear," Marmee said. "I'm sure Julia had a very good reason for it. And it relaxed all of us to hear it. You did a beautiful job."

Meg had her doubts about relaxing the wedding guests, but the song was sung and there was nothing she could do about it. Her one consolation was that she would never have to see Julia Thorpe again, except at such times that Lily Prescott Thorpe invited her over. And Julia might well be out of the house on those occasions.

Meg thought about apologizing to Lily for singing the wrong song, but the bride was so busy receiving all her guests, it didn't seem to be the right moment. Instead Meg stayed with her parents and helped herself to some of the food that had been set out.

"How I wish my other girls could be here,"

Marmee said. "To hear their sister sing, and then to see such a lovely ceremony."

"They'll have their own wedding days soon enough," Father said. "Oh, look. There's Julia Thorpe, standing by herself. Meg, why don't you bring her over so that we might meet her?"

Meg sighed but did as her father requested. Julia seemed surprised by Meg's invitation but followed her anyway. Meg made the introductions.

"You play the piano very well," Father said. "Have you studied long?"

"Since I was very little," Julia said. "William, my brother, feels it's important for a girl to have musical training."

"Our Bethy plays the piano," Marmee said. "And we all enjoy singing. Do you and your brother spend your evenings that way?"

"We used to," Julia said. "But now that he's taken a bride, I'm sure things will be different."

"And where will you be while they honeymoon?" Father asked. "I hear they plan to go to Niagara Falls."

"I'll be alone in our home," Julia said.

"With just the servants?" Marmee asked. "Oh, dear. How sad for you."

How sad for the servants, Meg thought.

"You must stay with us," Marmee said. "We'd be delighted to have you visit until your brother and Lily return from their honeymoon."

"Where will she stay?" Meg asked. Their house seemed crowded enough with just four girls.

"In your room," Marmee said. "You and Jo can certainly find space for another. Julia, let's ask your brother right away if he'll permit it, and if he does, you are our guest for as long as their honeymoon lasts!"

*I*t was a crowded carriage ride back to Julia's house. Neither Meg nor Julia did much talking. Mostly Mrs. Emerson and Marmee chatted about the wedding, while Meg stared at Julia and wondered how she was going to put up with such an unpleasant houseguest.

When they reached the Thorpes' house, Meg was even more troubled. It was as large as Aunt March's and just as forbidding. Julia entered, and Meg and Marmee followed. Julia seemed comfortable talking to the various servants, and Meg regretted even more Marmee's invitation to Julia. Surely Julia would be more comfortable staying in her lovely home, surrounded by caring servants, than she would be crowded into the March house with no one but Hannah to help with the housework.

Meg followed Julia to her bedroom and was immediately struck with envy. Julia's room was large and lovely, filled with dolls and books and toys. It was a finer room than even the bedrooms of Meg's wealthier friends, and it made the contrast between what Julia was accustomed to and what she was going to find at the Marches' even more striking.

"This is very kind of you, Mrs. March," Julia said as she and one of the maidservants gathered clothing for Julia to take with her. "I was going to feel lonely waiting for William's return."

"The girls will love having such a nice visitor," Marmee replied. "Won't they, Meg?"

Meg was busy fingering the lace curtains. She thought the lace was every bit as fine as Lily Thorpe's wedding gown. "Pardon?" she asked.

Marmee laughed. "Meg loves beautiful things," she said to Julia. "I'm sure she's wishing right now that her bedroom had such lovely curtains."

"Marmee," Meg protested, even though it was true.

"What our home does have is the sound of children laughing and playing," Marmee said. "You won't lack for companionship, Julia."

"I've always wished I had a sister," Julia said. "William is wonderful to me, but he's so much older, he's more like a father than a brother. Meg is very fortunate to have so many sisters."

"Just three," said Meg, who knew she was very fortunate but didn't care to have Julia Thorpe point it out to her. "And sometimes it can be very tiring having sisters."

"Now that Lily has married your brother, you do have a sister," Marmee said. "And one you'll grow to love. I'm sure you've packed enough for now, Julia. If you need anything else, we can have one of your servants bring it to us."

"May I bring one of my dolls?" Julia asked.

Marmee smiled. "Of course," she said. "Our Bethy has quite a collection. I'm sure she'd love to meet one of yours."

Julia examined several of her dolls before selecting one. "William gave me this one for my last birthday," she said.

"A good choice, then," Marmee said. "Come, girls. We've been keeping the others long enough."

The ride back to Concord was a long one. Meg spent much of it puzzling over Julia. She had seemed perfectly pleasant with Marmee, but Meg knew what a nasty person she really was. Meg wondered whether she should tell Marmee when the two of them were alone, but she decided not to. Marmee would surely see how ill-tempered Julia was, and then she'd appreciate even more Meg's good nature in putting up with her.

The Emersons dropped the Marches off at their home, and Father carried Julia's bag in with him. Meg looked at their house and worried more about Julia. The Marches' house was shabby compared to the Thorpes'. It was certain to bring out the surliness in Julia.

But Julia made no comments other than to thank Father for helping her with her bags. And when Jo, Beth, and Amy ran out of the house to greet them and demand details of the wedding, Julia merely stood aside and smiled at the commotion.

"Girls, we've brought you a surprise from the wedding," said Marmee. "This is Julia Thorpe, the groom's sister. We've invited her to stay with us until her brother and Lily are back from their honeymoon. Julia, these are our other little women, Jo and Beth and Amy."

Jo examined Julia carefully. Beth moved back, as she was always shy with strangers. But Amy reached out and took Julia's hand.

"I've never seen such a beautiful dress," Amy said. "Are all your clothes that pretty?"

Julia laughed. "This is my wedding dress," she said. "I'm afraid my other clothes are nowhere near as fancy."

Meg remembered what the clothes had

looked like when Julia had packed them and knew that they were far nicer than any she or her sisters owned. She waited for Julia to make a snide comment about what the March girls had on, but she didn't have the chance, because Amy was still speaking.

"Your dress is silk," she said. "Marmee, Julia's dress is silk. I thought young girls shouldn't wear silk."

"For special occasions such as a brother's wedding, silk is just the thing to wear," Marmee said. "Come, girls. Give Julia a chance to see our home. Jo, you and Meg will share your room with her."

"Capital," Jo said. "She can have my bed, and I'll sleep on the floor like a pioneer."

"Oh, no," Julia said. "I couldn't throw you out of your bed."

"Just for tonight, then," Jo said. "Tomorrow night we'll throw Meg out of hers!"

Beth and Amy both laughed, which only made Meg angrier.

"What a nice doll," Beth said as Julia carried it into the Marches' parlor. "Does she have a name?"

"No," Julia said. "I never thought to give her one. What do you think would be a good name for her?"

Beth examined the doll carefully. "She looks British," she declared. "Perhaps you should name her Victoria for the queen."

"Victoria it is, then," Julia said. "Thank you, Beth. I'm sure Victoria feels better having a name all her own."

"All my dolls have names," Beth said. "Do you think Victoria would care to meet them?"

"I'm sure she'd like that very much," Julia replied. "She's used to quite a bit of companionship, and she's probably lonely away from home."

"We can't have that," Marmee said. "Bethy, show Julia upstairs to her room, and then introduce Victoria to your dolls. Jo, tell Hannah there'll be one more for supper, and that Julia will be staying here for two weeks. Amy, stay with me and tell me all you girls did while we were gone. Meg, you help your father with Julia's bags, and then change into your every-day dress. We can't have your poplin getting dirty the very first time you wear it."

"Yes, Marmee," Meg said with a sigh. It was so unfair. Miserable, disagreeable Julia Thorpe got to wear her silk dress all day long, and not only did Meg have to take off her poplin, but she was also being made to carry Julia's bags, which were filled with the kind of clothing Meg only dreamed about.

She couldn't wait for Julia to reveal her true colors. Knowing she was bound to was the only comfort Meg had.

CHAPTER 5

" *H*ow did you sleep?" Julia asked Jo the next morning. "I worried about you all last night, sleeping on the floor."

Meg snorted. She couldn't imagine Julia worrying about putting anyone out.

"I see Meg's awake," Jo said. "She must have slept soundly, having a bed all to herself."

"I invited you to share it," Meg said. "You were the one who wanted to see what pioneer life was like."

"And now I've seen," Jo said. "I have to admit I'm glad I'm not a pioneer more often. Tonight we'll share."

"I can give up the bed," Julia said. "I'm sure I could survive being a pioneer for a single night."

"Marmee will figure something out," Meg said. "Perhaps she could borrow a mattress from one of our neighbors."

"Meg is so practical," Jo said with a yawn.

Meg wanted to deny it, but she suspected Jo was right. Besides, what was wrong with being practical? Given Jo's nature, it was probably best that Meg was.

The girls got up and dressed. Meg noted that Julia was wearing a dress not too dissimilar from the ones she and Jo had on, but Julia's was in perfect condition. Still, it wasn't silk, and Meg was grateful for that.

Amy bounded into the room. She still had her nightdress on. "May I wear it now?" she asked Julia.

"You certainly may," Julia replied.

"Wear what?" Meg asked, but neither Amy nor Julia bothered to answer. Instead Amy ran to where Julia had placed her bags and removed Julia's silk dress.

"Amy," Jo said.

"Julia said I could," Amy replied, and slipped the silk gown over her nightdress. "Oh, Julia, it's so beautiful. I feel so elegant in it, like a lady."

Beth entered the bedroom. Meg was relieved to see she was fully clothed. "You look like a princess," she said to Amy.

In Meg's opinion, Amy looked like a silly goose. Julia's dress was far too large for her.

"I'm wearing silk!" Amy sang. "Meg's only worn poplin!"

"This is my first silk dress," Julia said. "I'm sure I won't have another one for years."

"It's very nice of you to let Amy try it on," Meg said. "But I think she should take it off now, before she ruins it."

"I'm not going to ruin it," Amy said. "Can't I keep it on just a little longer, Julia?"

"Of course you can," Julia said. "Beth's right. You do look like a princess, Amy."

Amy danced around in the dress. Meg longed to try it on but vowed never to ask.

"I think that's enough," Jo said. "Amy, thank Julia and put on your own clothes."

Amy sighed but did as Jo instructed.

"It is fun to have sisters," Julia said. "If Amy were mine, I'd pet her and spoil her all the time."

"If she were yours, you'd tire of her soon enough," Meg said.

"Meg!" Beth said. "You sound just like Jo."

Jo and Amy both laughed. Meg managed to smile, but it wasn't easy.

The girls had breakfast. Then Jo announced her intention to work on her latest play. "It's called *The Lost Treasure of Captain Fortune*," she told Julia. "And it's absolutely capital."

"Don't use slang," Meg said automatically.

Jo grinned. "I use slang all the time," she told Julia.

"I don't know any slang," Julia said. "Perhaps you could teach me some."

"Oh, Meg will love that," Jo said. "But the play truly is capital. I play the captain, of course, as well as a wicked hag. Meg is going to play the princess, and Amy will play all the other parts."

"What will Beth do?" Julia asked, as though she really cared.

"I don't like to act," Beth said. "But I play the piano."

"That's right," Julia said. "Your mother told me that. Perhaps we could play a duet together."

"I'd like that," Beth said.

"Julia knows 'Lilly Dale,'" Meg said. "That's her best song."

"One of my best," Julia said. "But I'm sure I could read along with Beth's music. Do you want to play a song now?"

"Yes," Beth said. "Wait a moment. I'll be right back."

The girls went to the parlor and waited for Beth. She soon joined them, bringing her best doll from France with her.

"I thought Annabelle and Victoria might enjoy some conversation," Beth said to Julia.

"I'm sure they would." Julia went up to

Meg's room and brought Victoria downstairs. "Perhaps they could sit with us while we play the piano."

"I know Annabelle would like that," Beth said. "She's very musical."

The two girls sat in the center of the piano bench and carefully positioned Annabelle and Victoria on their laps. "What shall we play?" Julia asked Beth.

"Do you know 'Amazing Grace'?" Beth asked. "I've been practicing that a lot lately."

"I know it," Julia said. The girls began the hymn together.

Meg thought if she stayed there one more moment she would scream. "I'm going outside," she announced, but no one seemed to care. Jo went to the attic to do her writing. And Amy got her sketchpad and began drawing a picture of Julia and Beth at the piano.

Meg slowly left the room. How could it be, she wondered, that everyone liked Julia so and no one seemed to notice how unhappy Meg was about that?

CHAPTER 6

Ordinarily Meg enjoyed being out-doors, but ordinarily her sisters ac-companied her. This time Meg was on her own, and she knew it wouldn't be nearly as much fun. So she was relieved when she found her father working in their garden.

"Can I help, Father?" she asked. Meg didn't really like to garden, but she welcomed the opportunity to do something that would take her mind off the dreadful Julia.

"You can keep me company," Father re-plied. "There's no reason for both of us to get dirty. Hannah would prefer it if one of us stayed clean."

Meg smiled. Her father was always incredibly thoughtful.

"Where are your sisters?" Father asked. "And where is Julia?"

"They're all indoors," Meg said.

"Don't you want to be with them?" Father asked.

"I'd rather be here with you," Meg said. "Father, have you ever known a person who seemed one way but was really completely different?"

"I've known quite a few people like that in my day," replied Father.

"And they're bad people, aren't they?" Meg said, delighted to have found at least one person who understood.

"Sometimes," Father said. "Sometimes there are reasons for their behavior."

"What kind of reasons can there possibly be?" Meg asked. Surely Father knew just the sort of person Julia was, even though he might not realize that it was Julia she was talking about.

Father stood up and stretched. "Take Aunt March," he said.

"But Aunt March is always exactly the same," Meg said.

Father laughed. "That she is. But are you the same with her as you are with your sisters?"

"No, of course not," Meg said.

"Does that make you a bad person?" Father asked.

"That isn't fair," Meg said. "I'm more polite with Aunt March than I am with my sisters. But I try to be polite with them too. I'm just more so with Aunt March."

"Perhaps that isn't a good example," Father said. "Or perhaps you're too smart for me and I could never win a debate with you."

"You're the smartest person I know," Meg said. Surely her father was smart enough to see what sort of person Julia was. If he didn't disapprove so much of people who told tales, she'd admit it was Julia she was speaking of. "Father, I mean someone who is

41

not good but who appears that way," she said.

"Has this person committed great wrongs?" Father asked. "For example, is it someone who owns slaves but behaves courteously with people he regards as his equals?"

Meg thought about it. Forcing someone to sing "Lilly Dale" wasn't really in the same category as owning slaves. "Not great wrongs," she admitted. "But wrongs nonetheless."

"Sometimes we must be very kind to people who behave badly," Father said. "Sometimes they have a real need for our kindness."

That wasn't what Meg wanted to hear. "What if they don't deserve our kindness?" she asked. "What if they're deceitful and mean?"

"Then we try to behave as we would want them to," Father said. "And hope they can learn from our example."

"That isn't easy," Meg said.

"No," Father replied. "It isn't. And speaking of things that aren't easy, I see Aunt March coming up the walk."

"Oh, dear," said Meg, but then she smiled at the thought of Julia and Aunt March together.

"I think I'll spare both Aunt March and myself a discussion of whether it is proper for a gentleman to dirty himself growing vegetables," said Father. "You go in, Meg, and make my apologies to her for me."

"All right," Meg said, and she impulsively kissed her father's cheek. She only hoped none of the dirt on his face got onto hers; if it did, she knew she'd hear about it from Aunt March.

"What a pleasant surprise," Meg said to Aunt March as she joined her by the front gate. "Was Marmee expecting you?"

"I wasn't aware I needed an invitation," Aunt March said. "It's a pleasant day, and I was in the mood for a walk. Are your parents receiving?"

"Father sends his regrets," Meg said. "But Marmee is inside, and I'm sure she'll be delighted to visit with you."

Aunt March *humph*ed, but no more than usual.

"We have a visitor," Meg said. "Julia Thorpe is staying with us while her brother and Lily are on their honeymoon."

"At your age I knew nothing of honeymoons," Aunt March declared. "It's disgraceful the way children are being brought up these days."

"I'm sure it is, Aunt March," Meg said. She opened the door for her great-aunt and followed her into the parlor.

As always, Beth looked like a terrified deer at the sight of Aunt March. Amy, on the other hand, put down her sketchpad and ran over to greet her. And Julia stood and curtseyed.

"Very nicely done, I'm sure," Aunt March said. "Margaret, aren't you going to introduce me to this well-behaved young lady?"

"It's Julia Thorpe, Aunt March," Meg said. "The visitor I was just telling you about."

"That's hardly an introduction," Aunt March said. "Haven't you any manners at all, Margaret?"

"I'm sorry, Aunt March," Meg said. "This is Julia Thorpe."

Aunt March shook her head. "Sometimes I fear you are no better than heathens," she said. "Will one of you find your mother and tell her I am here?"

"I'll go," Beth said before Meg had the chance. Meg couldn't begrudge her the chance to escape.

Aunt March sat down. "Come here, Julia," she said. "I have some slight acquaintance with your brother."

"Do you, Mrs. March?" Julia asked, and her face lit up. Even Meg had to admit she was quite pretty when she wasn't scowling.

"I have that pleasure," Aunt March said. "Of course, I knew your parents better."

"Oh," Julia said. "It would be a wonderful kindness if you would tell me what you remember of them, Mrs. March. I love to hear them discussed, and I have so few opportunities to learn more about them."

"It would be my pleasure," Aunt March

said. "After I have visited with my niece, I'll sit with you. Your parents were very fine people, and I'm sure they would be quite proud of their daughter."

"Thank you, Mrs. March," Julia said. "I appreciate your kindness more than you can know."

Meg stared at Julia and Aunt March. Even Aunt March had fallen for Julia's act. Julia was even shrewder than Meg had imagined.

CHAPTER 7

J ulia and Aunt March seemed to talk forever. Meg told herself that she didn't
mind, that as long as Julia was occupied,
she could ignore her and concentrate on her
sewing. But even so, it was tedious sitting in
the parlor, hearing the two of them chatting
away.

When Aunt March finally prepared to leave,
she bent down and kissed Julia softly on her
forehead. "You are a delightful child," she pro-
claimed. "I hope Margaret and her sisters are
learning from your example."

"They have much to teach me," said Julia.

Meg rolled her eyes. Fortunately, Aunt

March didn't notice. Instead she said her farewells and left the house.

"Thank goodness that's over with," Meg said.

"You don't care for your aunt?" Julia asked.

Meg had no intention of discussing her feelings about Aunt March or anyone else with Julia. "Marmee," she said, "might I pay a visit to Mary Howe?"

"Do you know if she'd like that?" Marmee asked.

"I know she's home today," Meg said. "She told me I might come any day that she was home."

"Very well," Marmee said.

Meg smiled. Here was a wonderful way to rid herself of Julia.

"Might I come with you?" Julia asked.

"Of course you may," Marmee said. "Meg never meant to visit Mary and leave you behind. Did you, Meg, dearest?"

Meg felt her face turn red. "I don't know if Mary would like another visitor," she said.

"I'm sure she'd be delighted to meet Julia,"

Marmee said. "And it will be a nice treat for Julia to meet your friend. Go, girls, and have a good time."

Meg sighed, but if Julia or Marmee heard her, neither of them said anything. Instead Julia followed Meg outside.

"It's a lovely day," Julia said. "Does Mary Howe live far from here?"

"Not very far," Meg said. "But if you don't feel like walking, you certainly don't have to accompany me."

"I love walking," Julia said. "My brother and I took long walks regularly. Now I suppose he'll take them with his wife."

"Lily likes to walk," Meg said. "When she's visited, she's frequently taken strolls with us."

Julia didn't respond. Meg was just as happy not to have to speak to her, and the girls continued in silence.

Meg hoped Julia was impressed with Mary Howe's grand house. Mary's mother was as nice as she could be, but there was still something imposing about Mary's house, and Meg felt a little nervous whenever she went to call.

Mary's butler opened the door. "Meg March, come to visit with Mary," Meg said.

"This way, miss," the butler said, and he ushered Meg and Julia into the front parlor.

"Oh, dear," Meg said as the butler left to announce them. "I forgot to mention you were here also, Julia."

"Do you think Mary will mind?" Julia asked.

Meg was sure Mary wouldn't. "It's hard to say," she replied. "Mary is a true lady."

"Then I shall be on my best behavior," Julia said.

That was what Meg was afraid of. But before she had a chance to respond, Mary came bounding down the stairs and into the parlor.

"Meg!" she cried. "What a wonderful surprise. I've been longing for a visit from you."

For the first time that day, Meg felt good. "I would have come sooner if I'd been able to," she said to Mary. "But I've been so busy preparing for the wedding."

"I want to hear all about it," Mary said.

"Was it very grand? Was the bride the most beautiful in the world?"

"It was and she was!" Meg said, and she and Mary burst into laughter.

"But who's this?" Mary asked, looking at Julia.

"Julia Thorpe," Meg said. "Julia, this is my friend Mary."

"But the groom's name was Thorpe," Mary said.

"He's my brother," Julia said.

"Julia's staying with us while Lily is on her honeymoon," Meg said. "Otherwise she would have had to stay home alone with her servants."

"My parents travel a great deal, and they frequently leave my brother and me in the care of the servants," Mary said.

"I have no parents," Julia said.

"How sad," Mary said. "And how lonely for you. Are you close friends with the Marches? I don't remember Meg's ever mentioning you before."

51

"I only met them yesterday," said Julia. "Mr. and Mrs. March were kind enough to invite me to stay with them."

"They are the kindest people in the world," Mary said. "And Meg and her sisters are the most fun. Has Jo put on one of her plays for you yet?"

"Not yet," Julia said. "Perhaps before I leave."

"And how long will you be staying?" Mary asked.

"Two weeks," Julia replied. "Perhaps longer."

"Then I'm sure we'll have many opportunities to see each other," Mary said. "Meg, you will bring Julia with you when you come to call. I simply insist upon it."

"Jo is writing a new play now," Meg said. "She says it's quite the best thing she's ever written. I'm to play a beautiful princess."

"Maybe she could write a part for me," Julia said. "I haven't much experience play-acting, but I certainly would like to try."

Meg didn't know anyone better at playacting than Julia. "I'm sure Jo could work in something for you," she said. "I know there's a part for a vicious old hag."

"Meg!" Mary said. "Julia is far too pretty for such a part. Perhaps the princess could have a sister, and Julia could play that role."

"Jo will have to decide," Meg said. "But I doubt there's room in her play for two beautiful princesses."

"Jo is very clever," Mary said. "She'll work something out, Julia, I'm sure of it. Now tell me about the wedding. Do you love Lily, Julia? Is she like a sister to you?"

"She's been very kind to me," Julia replied. "And she was a beautiful bride."

Mary clapped her hands with delight. "Mama has just bought the most beautiful fashion magazine," she said. "Filled with pictures of dresses from Paris. Would you like to look at it, Julia?"

"I should love to," Julia said. "I've never seen a fashion magazine. My brother doesn't subscribe to any."

Mary laughed. "I wouldn't suppose a man

would," she said. "Come upstairs, Julia. The magazine is in my room, but I haven't had the chance to examine it yet. We'll look at all the pictures and imagine which dresses would look best on us."

"That does sound like fun," Meg said, but Mary didn't seem to hear her. Instead she had taken Julia's hand and led her up the stairs.

Meg followed them. She had known Mary Howe since they were both little girls, and she could never once remember Mary's holding her hand. Nor had Mary offered to look at a fashion magazine with her, even though Mary must know how much Meg would enjoy daydreaming about the clothing.

Meg loved Mary's bedroom. It was smaller than Julia's and didn't have quite so many splendid things, but it certainly was finer than any Meg had ever dreamed of living in.

"What a lovely room," Julia said as Mary showed them in. "How marvelous it must be to have a tree right outside one's window. It must make you feel as if you're sleeping in a magical forest."

54

Mary smiled. "It does sometimes," she said. "But often when the wind is blowing, the branches hit my window, and I get terribly frightened."

"My brother used to comfort me when there was a storm," Julia said. "But now I suppose he'll comfort Lily instead."

"Lily isn't frightened of storms," Meg said. Lily had never seemed to her the sort to be frightened of anything.

"Thunder and lightning used to terrify me," Mary said. "When I was very little, that is."

"Me too!" exclaimed Julia, and she and Mary laughed. "How silly we were when we were little."

"I was always more afraid when my parents weren't home," Mary said. "My brother, Willie, isn't much for comforting."

"Your brother is named William?" Julia asked. "So is mine!"

"Oh, but that's too amazing," Mary said. "Both of us with brothers and both named William."

"I know lots of people named William,"

Meg muttered. It wasn't as though they both had brothers named Oglethorpe, after all.

"Still, it's quite something," said Mary. "Though *your* brother William sounds much kinder than mine."

"He has always been kindness itself to me," said Julia.

"But have you ever wished for a sister?" Mary asked. "I know I have many times."

"William has been family enough for me," Julia replied. "He's been like a mother and a father. I've never felt the need for a sister."

"One doesn't feel the need for them," Meg said. "One simply has them foisted upon one."

Mary laughed. "How you talk, Meg," she said. "As though three little sisters were the same as one older brother."

"Meg is very fortunate," Julia said, "to have loving parents."

"And ones who don't travel," Mary said. "Meg, you cannot possibly know what loneliness is."

"What I should like to know is what fashion is," Meg said, thoroughly tired of this talk of brothers and loneliness. "Where is your mother's magazine, Mary?"

"Right here," Mary said, and opened it at random to a picture of a dark green silk day dress.

"Oh, how beautiful that is," Julia said.

"It would be perfect with your coloring," Mary said. "The dress could have been designed for you, Julia."

"And this one for you, Mary," Julia said, pointing to a rich burgundy-colored silk evening gown. "How magnificent you would look in it."

"Yes, I would, rather," Mary said, and burst into peals of laughter. "I can just imagine what Mama would say if I asked for such a gown."

"Not now, perhaps," Julia said. "But after you're married, you'll own many such beautiful dresses."

"And you will also," Mary said. "Poor Meg."

"Pardon?" Meg said. She had been dreaming of owning a gown as splendid as the burgundy one, which would go perfectly with her coloring as well. "What about me?"

"Unless you marry money, you'll never be able to afford such fine dresses," Mary said. "I know one shouldn't speak of money, but it is such a dreadful shame your family doesn't have any."

Julia looked at Meg, who blushed, then grew angry at herself for blushing and turned even redder. "Meg's pretty enough," Julia said. "I'm sure she could make a good match."

"I would never marry just for money," Meg said.

"Then you'll simply have to become a seamstress and make such fine gowns for yourself," Julia said. "Oh, Mary, look at this one." And she pointed to a gray plaid morning dress.

"Mama has one almost like that," Mary said.

Meg looked at the dress. Marmee had nothing nearly as splendid. And Aunt March, who had the money for such fine clothes, didn't approve of wasting money on them.

Meg watched as Mary and Julia pored over

the magazine, analyzing each dress. She would never own anything so fine.

It was all so unfair. Meg worked hard at being good, and she had nothing. Julia, who was nasty and mean, had money and position, and now she even had Meg's best friend to call her own.

CHAPTER 8

*M*eg and Julia walked home together. Julia was full of chatter about Mary and how nice she was, and how pretty all the gowns in the magazine had been. Meg hardly bothered listening. She thought if she had to spend another minute in Julia's company she would scream.

When they finally reached the Marches' house, Meg stopped before stepping up to the door. "I'm going for a walk," she declared. "By myself."

"All right," said Julia. "I'll see you later."

Meg knew that was true and there was nothing she could do about it. But she seized the chance for some privacy and took a long walk through the apple orchards of Concord.

As she walked, she imagined herself married to a man of great wealth and position. Surely there was one such man whom she could love. Lily had found such a man for herself, although if William Thorpe was anything like his disagreeable sister, Meg felt sorry for Lily.

Meg knew Aunt March wanted her to make a good match, for that would help her sisters make fine society marriages as well. But Meg also knew that the happiest couple in the world was Marmee and Father, and they had far more love than riches.

Burgundy silk evening dresses would remain a fantasy even when Meg was old enough to own one. Julia might have a closet full of them, but Meg would have none. It was so miserably unfair.

"Good things should happen to good people," Meg said out loud. Perhaps someday there would be a prince or a duke or an earl who was looking for a girl such as she to be his bride. Stranger things had happened, she supposed, although she didn't know what they could have been.

By the time Meg got home, she was almost in a good mood. True, Julia was still there, but by now Jo and Beth and Amy must surely have seen through Julia's act, and Meg at least would have the satisfaction of listening to them complain about their unpleasant house guest.

She found Beth and Marmee mending. Annabelle and Victoria sat beside them. "Did you have a nice walk?" Marmee asked.

"Yes, I did," Meg said. "Where are the others?"

"Jo's in the attic working on her play," Marmee replied. "And Julia and Amy are in the kitchen helping Hannah."

"Amy is helping Hannah?" Meg asked. Amy never did anything around the house unless she was absolutely forced to.

Marmee laughed. "Julia said she wanted to learn how to cook," she said. "And Amy would follow Julia to the ends of the earth. I believe Hannah is giving them lessons in peeling potatoes."

"I already know how to peel potatoes," Beth said. "Otherwise I'd be with Julia too. She's so nice, I'm not afraid of her at all."

"I can't imagine Amy peeling potatoes," Meg said. "I think I'll go to the kitchen and see this for myself."

"I don't blame you," Marmee said, and burst out laughing again.

Meg walked to the kitchen. Sure enough, Julia and Amy both had knives in their hands and were bent over a pile of potatoes while Hannah instructed them on the finer points of peeling.

Julia looked up as Meg entered the room. "This is so much fun," she said. "I'm never allowed in the kitchen back home. And I do think knowing how to cook is terribly important. Don't you, Meg?"

"Terribly," Meg said. "Are you enjoying yourself, Amy?"

"When I grow up I'm going to be a lady and

wear beautiful silk dresses all day long," Amy replied. "I don't think you can cook wearing silk. Can you, Hannah?"

"I'm sure I wouldn't know," Hannah said, "never having worn silk."

"I have," Amy said. "Today I've worn silk and peeled potatoes. I'd rather wear silk."

Julia laughed as though Amy had said the funniest thing. "You're such a clever little dear," she said. "Isn't she, Meg?"

"Oh, yes," Meg said. "She's very clever." *Not clever enough to see through Julia,* she thought.

"I don't see you offering to help with the potatoes, Meg," Hannah said. "There's plenty here for you to do."

"I have other work to keep me busy," Meg said, hoping no one would ask her just what. "Have fun peeling potatoes." What was most annoying was they did seem to be having fun.

Meg went to her room. She didn't often have a chance to simply sit there by herself. There was school to go to and chores to do

and all the games she and her sisters enjoyed playing.

This will be nice, she told herself. No one would disturb her. She could think her own private thoughts.

But all her thoughts were angry ones. Now even Hannah thought Julia was wonderful. And Marmee would never get over Amy's peeling potatoes simply because Julia was doing it.

Meg found she didn't like sitting by herself. No wonder she never did it. For lack of any-place else to go, she went upstairs to the attic. Sure enough, Jo was bent over her makeshift desk, hard at work on *The Lost Treasure of Captain Fortune.*

"Your timing is perfect," Jo said. "I've just finished making changes to my play."

"What changes?" Meg asked. Surely Jo hadn't created another beautiful princess.

"You'll see," Jo said, and grabbed Meg's hand. "Let's go downstairs and get the others. I want to tell them all about their new parts."

"New parts?" Meg asked, but she followed Jo down the steps.

Jo called for Amy, Beth, and Julia, and soon the girls were gathered in the parlor.

"Excuse me, my dear," Marmee said, rising to leave the room. "Aunt March's visit has put me behind on all my work today."

"Thank you, Marmee," Jo said. "She knows I don't like my rehearsals to be open to the public," she said to Julia. "Marmee is such a brick."

"Don't use slang," Meg said.

"That's just the tone I want you to use in your part," Jo said. "I knew this recasting would work wonderfully well."

"What recasting?" Meg asked. "I play the beautiful princess. And I'm sure princesses don't care for slang either."

Jo laughed. "You're probably right," she said. "But you're not the princess any longer. Julia is."

Amy clapped her hands. "Oh, that's perfect, Jo," she said. "Julia was born to play a princess."

"But that's my part," Meg said.

"I've written you just as good a part," Jo said. "Don't worry, Meg. Julia, you will play the princess, won't you? The play wouldn't be nearly as good without you."

"If you think I could," Julia said. "I have no experience acting."

"Neither did any of us when we first began," Jo said. "Amy's only been in our plays a few months herself, but already she's handling many parts."

"Someday I'll get to play the princess," Amy said.

Julia smiled. "You should already. Why not have Amy play the princess, Jo? She'd probably do as well as I would."

"She's not ready yet," said Jo. "But, Julia, I'm sure you'll be perfectly grand. And you have the dress for it. Seeing Amy in your dress this morning gave me the idea. None of us could even remotely resemble a princess with the clothes we own."

"I'm flattered," Julia said. "I'd certainly love to try."

"Julia, you'll be just wonderful," Beth said. "I'll play the piano for you, and you can sing a song. Can't she, Jo?"

"Absolutely," Jo said. "Any song that Julia cares to sing. As long as it's a princessy sort of song."

"And just who am I to play?" Meg said. She was the one who usually got to sing in Jo's plays. But then she always got to play the princess too.

"The wicked hag!" Jo exclaimed. "Now that I don't have to play the part as well as that of noble Captain Fortune, the hag can be a far larger role. Oh, Meg, you'll be the best hag I can imagine. You do all sorts of terrible things to poor Julia here. The audience will loathe you!"

"But couldn't there be two princesses?" Meg asked. "One good and one wicked?"

"Perhaps in some other play," said Jo. "But in this one there is one princess and one ugly hag. Meg, you're always saying how much you like to act, and how you want bigger, more challenging parts. Now I've written one just for you. We'll dress you in the most awful rags and make you look as ugly as ugly can be. And when I kill you at the end, and Julia is rescued from your evil doings, the audience will simply go mad with pleasure."

"Only if I don't go mad first!" Meg cried. She ran from the parlor and away from her sisters, who had once loved her and now loved Julia instead.

CHAPTER 9

*M*eg sat under the winter apple tree and wept. No one loved her. Jo thought of her as a hag, and neither Beth nor Amy seemed to disagree. Instead they went on about how perfect a princess Julia would be.

Meg stopped crying when she grew angry again. It was unjust that Julia should be loved so. How could it be that no one, not Jo or Beth or Amy or Mary or Aunt March or Hannah or even Marmee or Father, could see Julia for what she was?

For the first time in Meg's life, she thought about running away. Then her family would realize who the good child was. Then they would realize that it was Julia who had driven Meg away, and they'd turn on her and restore Meg to her proper place as the oldest, much-loved daughter of the March family.

It was a comforting fantasy, even though Meg knew it was as likely to come to pass as her marrying a prince. In the meantime, she could stay under the apple tree and continue to feel angry and sorry for herself.

"There you are."

Meg turned around.

"I've been looking for you," Julia said. "Jo wanted to talk to you, but I thought it might be better if I did."

"I have nothing to say to you," Meg sniffed.

"Good," Julia said. "Then I'll speak and you'll listen. It's probably better that way."

Meg shook her head. "You should play the princess," she said. "You are the most over-bearing girl I've ever met."

Julia sat down on the ground next to Meg. "I suppose I would seem that way to you," she said. "You've seen me at my worst, Meg. But

I'm terribly grateful to you, and this is the first chance I've had to tell you that."

"Grateful to me?" Meg asked. "Why?"

"Because you haven't told everybody how awful I was yesterday," Julia replied. "At William's wedding. If you had, I'm sure nobody would like me."

"At least you admit it," Meg said. "Making me sing 'Lilly Dale' like that."

Julia nodded. "William didn't tell me to play that," she said. "He knew I was to play something; Lily told him that, but she wouldn't say what. She asked me to play 'Amazing Grace,' and she told me you'd be singing it. I rehearsed it all week, whenever William was out of the house."

"So why did you insist on 'Lilly Dale' instead?" Meg asked. "Just to embarrass me?"

"No, of course not," Julia said. "I didn't even know you. Why should I care if you were embarrassed?"

Meg realized that the Julia she'd met the day before really wouldn't have cared if she was embarrassed, and she would have done

73

nothing to prevent it from happening. "You're supposed to care," she informed Julia. "You're supposed to not want people to feel embarrassed."

"Oh," Julia said. "Oh, I see what you mean. I was dreadful yesterday, wasn't I?"

"Yes," Meg said, "you certainly were."

"I'm sorry, Meg," Julia said. "It's Lily. I mean, it isn't Lily, not really. I hardly know her. William says she's wonderful. He talks about her all the time, how sweet she is, how kind."

"She is," Meg said. "I've never heard her say a cross word."

"But William is all I have," Julia said. "You can't imagine what that's like. You have your parents and three sisters. My parents died when I was a baby. I hardly even remember them. And William gave up everything to take care of me. I thought we'd be together forever, but then he met Lily and I saw less and less of him. When he told me they planned to be married, I thought I would die. Lily was sure to want me out of

the house. I didn't know what was to become of me. I still don't, not really."

"That's terrible," Meg said, and for the first
time since meeting Julia, she actually sympa-
thized with her.

"I probably made things worse by having
you sing that dreadful song," Julia said. "William hates it, because Lilly Dale dies. I don't
know. I just thought maybe if he heard it right
before the wedding, he'd change his mind and
not marry her after all."

"That was a very bad plan," Meg said.

"I know," Julia said with a sigh. "And now
he's married her anyway, and I don't know
what he'll say when he returns from his honeymoon. About the song. About where I'm going to live. About anything. And you've been
so nice. I feel dreadful."

"I don't think I've been as nice as all that,"
said Meg.

"You haven't been," Julia said. "But your
family certainly has."

"Of course they were nice," Meg said.
"They're nice people. And besides, you've

been acting like a perfect angel since you got here. Playing duets. Petting Amy. Peeling potatoes."

"I thought perhaps if I behaved myself, your parents might let me live here," Julia said. "They are such kind people, and I have always wanted sisters."

"No," Meg said. "I mean, even if we wanted to, there's no room for you here. And Marmee and Father don't have a lot of money."

"Oh, I'm sure William would be most happy to help out," Julia said. "He'll probably board me out somewhere anyway. Why not here? Your family is respectable. I'm sure they'd see to it that I got a good education. And I wouldn't live so far away from William that I'd never see him. Perhaps he and Lily would let me visit at Christmas."

Meg thought about it. She knew of families who took in boarders, and her parents could certainly use the extra income. She still wasn't sure whether she liked Julia, but at least she could understand her better now.

"I don't know where we'd put you," Meg

said. "But perhaps we could turn the attic into a bedroom for Jo. She spends most of her time there anyway."

"Then we would share this room," Julia said. "Oh, Meg, I'd like that so much. I'd let you wear my silk dress anytime you wanted."

Meg pictured herself in Julia's lovely dress. She knew it would look absolutely splendid on her. "My sisters do seem to have taken to you," she said. "Jo thinks you're capital, and Beth said you were very nice. Amy peeled potatoes for you. They wouldn't mind if you came to stay."

"You'll like me too," Julia said. "I'll do anything you want, Meg, if you just let me live here with you."

"All right," Meg said. "I won't tell anybody about how wretched you were yesterday. But of course it's up to Father and Marmee to decide if you should live here."

"Let's ask your mother right now," Julia said.

"Why hurry?" Meg asked.

Julia smiled. "I've been on my very best behavior since I arrived here," she said. "I don't know how long I can continue to act this way. I really don't care for slang words. And I've never wanted to learn how to peel potatoes."

"I'm glad to hear that," said Meg. "Very well. Let's find Marmee and see what she thinks."

The girls went downstairs. Marmee was in the parlor reading. Meg was glad to find her alone.

"Hello, dears," Marmee said. "Julia, have you been enjoying your stay with us?"

"Oh, yes," Julia said. "Very much."

"That's what we've come to talk to you about," Meg said. "Marmee, Julia's been having such a good time here. And everyone likes her so much."

"Yes, that's true," Marmee said. "Even Hannah has told me what a sweet girl you are, Julia. And words of praise from Hannah are to be cherished."

"That's why we were thinking perhaps Julia should move in with us," Meg said. "We were just discussing it outside."

"But Julia has a fine home with her brother," Marmee said. "You're happy there, aren't you, dear?"

"Oh, yes," Julia said. "That is, I always have been. But things are different now. I'm sure William would be most glad to pay for my upkeep. And I'm quite well behaved. I'd be so quiet, you'd hardly know I was here."

"It sounds as though you've given this a great deal of thought," Marmee said. "Meg, what do you think of Julia's plan?"

Meg wasn't sure herself. But then she remembered how helpful it would be to the Marches to have additional income. And there was that silk dress to consider. "I think it could work out well," she said. "And it would be a help to all around."

"My," Marmee said. "Such an ambitious plan. Julia, you've been here only a day. Surely we're not so wonderful that you'd be willing to give up your own family for ours."

"I have no family," Julia said. "I had a brother, but he's married now, and his family consists of him and his new bride. I'm alone in this world, Mrs. March, and I have nowhere else to turn. I promise I'll be good, if you'll just let me live here." Much to Meg's horror, Julia began to cry.

Marmee reached out to Julia and embraced her. "There, there, child," she murmured. "It will be all right."

"But what if it isn't?" Julia asked. "I did a terrible thing at William's wedding. He might never wish to see me again. And Lily will never forgive me. I'm sure of that."

"What did you do?" Marmee asked.

"I made Meg sing 'Lilly Dale,'" Julia said, and she burst into fresh tears.

Marmee laughed. "I'm sorry, dear," she said, stroking Julia's hair. "I know that seems like a dreadful thing to have done, but I doubt William will disown you for it."

"It's not William I'm so worried about." Julia sniffed. "It's Lily. She must think I'm terrible. She'll never want me in her home."

"I think you're wrong there," Marmee said. "Of course, you should apologize to both Wil-

liam and Lily when they return. I trust you've already apologized to Meg."

"She has," Meg said. "And I've forgiven her." She realized with a start that she had indeed forgiven Julia, and she even felt sorry for her.

Marmee reached into her pocket and handed Julia her handkerchief. "If William and Lily should decide you ought to make your home elsewhere, my husband and I will be more than happy to discuss various possibilities with them," she said. "But I doubt it will come to that. Lily is a kind and loving girl, and I'm sure she will come to love you as a sister."

"Do you really think so?" Julia asked.

"I do," Marmee said. "I'm convinced that once you get to know her, you'll love her as my daughters do. And then you'll rejoice in William's marriage."

"I have an idea," said Meg. "Why doesn't Julia stay here for a day or two after William and Lily return from their honeymoon? We can invite them to dinner. That way Julia

82

won't feel quite so alone when she greets them and apologizes to them."

"Oh, could I?" Julia asked.

"You certainly could," Marmee said. "And what's more, we won't even make you peel the potatoes!"

CHAPTER 10

" *I*'m so nervous," Julia admitted the night of the dinner party. "Do you think everything will go well?"

"It will be positively capital," said Jo.

"Don't use slang," Meg said. "But I think it will be capital too, Julia."

The girls examined everything in the dining room one last time. There were candles on the table, although it stayed light so late into the evening there was little need for them. Amy and Beth had picked armloads of daisies, and the room had several vases of them. The table was set with Marmee's best china and silver. Meg was wearing her new poplin, and even Jo's dress was respectably free of ink stains.

"Jo, do pretend to be William once again," Julia said. "And Meg, you be Lily. It's so important I apologize to them just right."

"Very well," Jo said. "Julia, you caused me great pain at my wedding."

"Yes, William, I know," Julia said. "And I beg you and Lily to forgive me."

"I forgive you," Meg said.

"No," Jo said. "You must be harsher, Meg."

"But Lily isn't harsh," Meg said. "And I'm sure she's forgiven Julia already."

"Then I'll be harsh," Jo said. "Julia, what you did was despicable. How's that for a word? I only learned it the other day. And I'm determined that all my villains will be despicable from now on."

"I doubt that William cares how your villains will be," said Meg. "Julia, I'm sure a simple apology will do. And we've rehearsed this one as often as I rehearsed 'Amazing Grace.' "

"With better results, I hope," Jo said. "Oh, I think I hear them coming."

Jo was right. The girls ran to the window and saw William and Lily alighting from their carriage.

"Their arms are filled with presents," Jo said. "That must be a good sign."

Julia ran out to greet her brother. Meg followed and watched as William swooped down to embrace his sister. Lily hugged Julia as well.

"Oh, it's so good to be home," Lily said. "And Julia, we can hardly wait for you to return with us."

"The house isn't the same without you," William said.

"But I have to apologize first," Julia said. "William, Lily, I'm most dreadfully sorry I ruined your wedding day."

"You did?" William asked. "Lily, dearest, did you notice our wedding day ruined in any way?"

"I thought the day was perfect," Lily said. "What did you do, Julia, that has you so upset?"

"I made Meg sing 'Lilly Dale,' " Julia declared, "instead of 'Amazing Grace' the way you wanted, Lily. It was a terrible thing for me to have done. Can you ever forgive me?"

"This is a most grave offense," William said. " 'Lilly Dale.' You know how I feel about that song, Julia."

Julia nodded. "I'm so sorry," she said. "Please forgive me. I'll never do anything that wicked again."

"William, darling, stop teasing the poor child," Lily said. "Julia, William and I were oblivious to everything that day except each other. I wouldn't have noticed if you'd played 'God Save the Queen.' And I like 'Lilly Dale.' It's flattering to have a song with my name in it. Could you play it for us this evening, do you think? I know all the words, and I'd love to sing along."

"You really don't mind?" Julia asked.

"I think if that's the wickedest thing you ever do, the world will be a safe place indeed," William said. "Now, how about if we go inside so that we can share all our fine souvenirs of Niagara Falls with you and the Marches?"

"Oh, yes," said Jo. "I'd love to see things from Niagara Falls."

Julia walked between her brother and Lily. Meg noticed how happy the three of them seemed to be and decided it was unlikely that Julia would be coming to live with the Marches. She regretted for a moment the loss of the silk dress and the extra income, but she was glad for Julia and for herself too. It had been crowded in her bedroom, and Jo had been reluctant to sleep in the attic on hot summer nights.

Dinner was a great success. Lily was especially impressed when Julia declared that she had helped to prepare it. "Hannah's been teaching me how to cook," Julia said. "I've learned how to peel potatoes and boil eggs and roast meats."

"I offered to teach her how to pluck chickens, but that she turned down," Hannah said.

"Perhaps on my next visit," Julia said, and everyone laughed.

After dinner, the girls staged *The Lost Treasure of Captain Fortune*. Julia played the princess, but Meg's part, the hag, had been improved somewhat when Jo had decided the hag too had been put under an evil spell. Once she had been released from it through Captain Fortune's slaying of a dragon (played none too convincingly by Amy), it turned out that the hag was no hag at all, but Captain Fortune's mother, who happened to have the key to the lost treasure. Father, Marmee, William, Lily, and Hannah all agreed it was the best play they'd seen in many a month.

"I'll miss you all so fiercely," Julia said as she exchanged farewells with the Marches. William and Lily were standing by the carriage, waiting for Julia to join them. "You've shown me what a family can truly be like."

"You'll learn to love your new family," Marmee said. "And we will always be here if you should need or want us."

"I know that," Julia said, giving Marmee a final hug. "Good-bye, everyone. I love you all."

"We love you too," Amy said. "And when you outgrow your silk dress, think of me!"

"Amy!" Meg said, but the others just laughed. Julia got into the carriage and waved good-bye as she began her journey home.

Meg stood with her family outside their house for a moment. The sun had not yet begun to set, and she could see them all clearly. They were the best family in the world, she thought. And she knew that no matter where her life took her, she would always cherish being a member of the Marches.

PORTRAITS OF LITTLE WOMEN ACTIVITIES

BUTTERMILK
COFFEE CAKE

This prizewinning delight is scrumptious for breakfast, brunch, or afternoon tea. It can be served at room temperature or warm. Either way it's a tasty treat.

INGREDIENTS
   1 cup white sugar
   ¾ cup brown sugar (light or dark)
   1 teaspoon ground cinnamon
   2½ cups flour, sifted
   1 teaspoon baking powder
   1 teaspoon baking soda
   1 cup buttermilk
   ¾ cup corn oil
   1 egg, beaten
   1 cup chopped walnuts (or pecans)

Preheat oven to 350 degrees.
Grease and flour a 9-by-13-by-2-inch pan.

1. Mix sugars and cinnamon. Set aside ³/₄ cup for topping.
2. Sift flour with baking powder.
3. Dissolve baking soda in buttermilk.
4. Add flour mixture, buttermilk, oil, and egg to remaining sugar-cinnamon mixture. Stir only until well mixed. Do not beat.
5. Pour into greased and floured baking pan.
6. Add nuts to reserved sugar-cinnamon mixture and blend.
7. Sprinkle this mixture on top of cake batter. Take a knife and cut the mixture into the batter, using a swirling motion.
8. Bake in preheated oven about 25 minutes, or until a toothpick inserted into center of cake comes out dry.

Let cake cool. Cut into 12 pieces.

PINCUSHION

This lovely pincushion can be made plain or fancy. The fancy version—with satin or lace or both—adds a decorative touch to a dresser or nightstand. A simpler version, made from felt or calico, is a pretty and very functional addition to any sewer's basket of notions.

MATERIALS

2 ounces of polyester fiberfill or any soft material for core

4 yards of yarn

1 10-inch circle of polyester or cotton batting

Long straight pins

Long needle and thread

6- or 7-inch square of decorative fabric to cover bottom

14-inch circle of decorative fabric for cover
(same fabric as for bottom)
18-inch circle of lacy material for outer
cover
1/2 yard of satin ribbon, 1/4-inch wide
Decorative straight pins

PINCUSHION

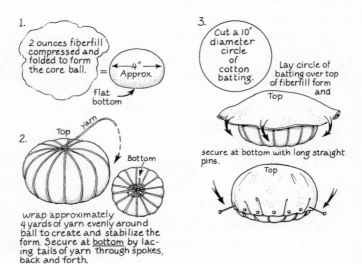

1.
2 ounces fiberfill compressed and folded to form the core ball.

= 4" Approx.

Flat bottom

2.
Top

yarn

Bottom

wrap approximately 4 yards of yarn evenly around ball to create and stabilize the form. Secure at <u>bottom</u> by lacing tails of yarn through spokes, back and forth.

3.
Cut a 10" diameter circle of cotton batting.

Lay circle of batting over top of fiberfill form and

Top

secure at bottom with long straight pins.

Top

4.

Cut a 6"or 7" square of decorative fabric to cover flat bottom.

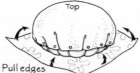

Pull edges up all around and, using long straight pins, pin in place.

5.

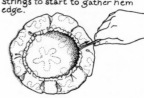

1½ yards of yarn →

Cut a 14" diameter circle of decorative material (same as for bottom) Sew ¼" or ⅜" hem all around, enclosing (but not sewing into!) 1½-yard-long piece of yarn to be used as a drawstring. Pin hem in place before sewing.

Tail ends of yarn

Closeups

cross section

6. After hemming all around,

remove pins, pull on yarn drawstrings to start to gather hem edge.

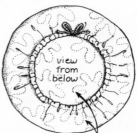

7.

fit cover over form, and when snugly and evenly fit, tie a knot or bow with

→ (pull tight)

yarn tails; trim off excess.

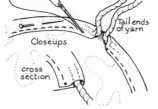

view from below

Note: matching materials

97

8.

Cut an 18" diameter circle of lacy material for outer cover.

Sew a ⅜" hem around the lacy fabric. (for a neater edge fold the raw edge under, then fold again and hem.)

side view cross section

---- raw edge

This hem will actually be used as the drawstring, so the entire circle of hem must stay unbroken. Don't make the stitches too small or the thread may break when you gather it. You can use doubled thread.

Pull smoothly and gently to gather.

9. The gathered hem of this lacy outer cover will be at the top of the cushion to make a ruffle.

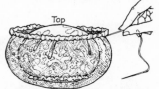

Top

Pull the drawstring thread tight, enclosing the cushion form. The pattern of the inner cover will be partially visible through the lacy outer cover.

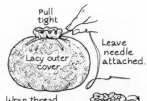

Pull tight

Lacy outer cover.

Leave needle attached.

Wrap thread tightly around neck, then sew through once or twice and cut off thread.

10.

Tie a ribbon bow around the neck of the ruffled top, leaving 4" tails after making bow.

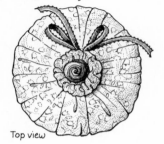

Decorate with a ribbon rose, special button, or whatever suits your fancy!

Top view

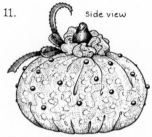

11. Side view

You can decorate the cushion with real straight pins and needles.

You may choose to make several pincushions. And whether plain or fancy, they make a lovely teacher's gift or a present for your best friend.

ABOUT THE AUTHOR OF PORTRAITS OF LITTLE WOMEN

SUSAN BETH PFEFFER is the author of both middle-grade and young adult fiction. Her middle-grade novels include *Nobody's Daughter* and its companion, *Justice for Emily*. Her highly praised *The Year Without Michael* is an ALA Best Book for Young Adults, an ALA YALSA Best of the Best, and a *Publishers Weekly* Best Book of the Year. Her novels for young adults include *Twice Taken*, *Most Precious Blood*, *About David*, and *Family of Strangers*. Susan Beth Pfeffer lives in Middletown, New York.

A WORD ABOUT LOUISA MAY ALCOTT

LOUISA MAY ALCOTT was born in 1832 in Germantown, Pennsylvania, and grew up in the Boston-Concord area of Massachusetts. She received her early education from her father, Bronson Alcott, a renowned educator and writer, who eventually left teaching to study philosophy. To supplement the family income, Louisa worked as a teacher, a household servant, and a seamstress, and she wrote stories as well as poems for newspapers and magazines. In 1868 she published the first volume of *Little Women*, a novel about four sisters growing up in a small New England town during the Civil War. The immediate success of *Little Women* made Louisa May Alcott a celebrated writer, and the novel remains one of today's best-loved books. Alcott wrote until her death in 1888.